Dear Parent:
Your child's love of reading starts here!

Every child learns to read in a different way and at his or her own speed. Some go back and forth between reading levels and read favorite books again and again. Others read through each level in order. You can help your young reader improve and become more confident by encouraging his or her own interests and abilities. From books your child reads with you to the first books he or she reads alone, there are I Can Read Books for every stage of reading:

SHARED READING
Basic language, word repetition, and whimsical illustrations, ideal for sharing with your emergent reader

BEGINNING READING
Short sentences, familiar words, and simple concepts for children eager to read on their own

READING WITH HELP
Engaging stories, longer sentences, and language play for developing readers

READING ALONE
Complex plots, challenging vocabulary, and high-interest topics for the independent reader

ADVANCED READING
Short paragraphs, chapters, and exciting themes for the perfect bridge to chapter books

I Can Read Books have introduced children to the joy of reading since 1957. Featuring award-winning authors and illustrators and a fabulous cast of beloved characters, I Can Read Books set the standard for beginning readers.

A lifetime of discovery begins with the magical words **"I Can Read!"**

Visit www.icanread.com for information on enriching your child's reading experience.

To Avi
—S.W.

To Aunt Anne with love
—J.M.

www.icanread.com

Library of Congress Cataloging-in-Publication Data
Weeks, Sarah.
Mac and Cheese / by Sarah Weeks ; pictures by Jane Manning.—1st ed.
p. cm.—(I can read)
Summary: Two cats that are as different as night and day are nevertheless best friends.
ISBN 978-0-06-117079-9 (trade bdg.) — ISBN 978-0-06-117081-2 (pbk.)
[1. Stories in rhyme. 2. Best friends—Fiction. 3. Friendship—Fiction. 4. Individuality—Fiction. 5. Cats—Fiction.]
I. Manning, Jane K., ill. II. Title.
PZ8.3.W4125Mac 2010 2008014199
[E]—dc22 CIP
AC

21 22 23 CWM 30 29 28 27 ❖ First Edition

BY **Sarah Weeks**

ILLUSTRATED BY **Jane Manning**

LAURA GERINGER BOOKS
An Imprint of HarperCollins*Publishers*

FISH
MARKET

Macaroni likes to eat.

He isn't very picky.

But Cheese will never take a bite

of anything that's icky.

“This fish is cold and very old.
I do not like fish old and cold.”

But Macaroni eats the fish,

then licks his lips and says, “Delish!”

"Nice day," says Mac.

Cheese says, "Too hot."

“Let’s swim,” says Mac.

Cheese says, “Let’s not.”

Macaroni finds a hat.

It’s very blue and very flat.

“I like this hat,” says Mac.

“Do you?”

Cheese frowns and says,
“Too flat. Too blue.”

Too cold, too flat,

too this, too that.

Too old, too blue,

too, too, too, too.

Macaroni likes to jump.

Cheese just sits there like a lump.

Macaroni likes to play.

Cheese says, “Mac, please go away!”

When Macaroni sings a song,
Cheese will never sing along.

Mac likes to jump and play and sing,
but Cheese does not like anything.

Bouncing? Nope.

Pouncing? Nope.

Flipping? Nope.

Skipping rope?

Mac thinks chasing mice is fun.

Cheese says,

“Wake me when you’re done.”

"What's wrong with you?"

Mac asks one day.

"Why don't you ever want to play?

Why won't you pounce

or bounce or jump?

Why are you such a grumpy grump?

I like to flip and skip and sing,

but Cheese, you don't like anything."

Cheese says, “It’s true, I am a grump.
I do not like to skip or jump,
or bounce or pounce or swim or play
or chase a mouse around all day.

The only thing I like to do
is sit here quietly with you.”

Mac feels so good when he hears that,

he jumps for joy and throws his hat.

The wind blows! Away it goes!

“Oh no! There goes my hat!” cries Mac.

Cheese says, “Mac, I’ll get it back.”

To get that hat Cheese has to pounce

and run and jump and swim and bounce.

He has to skip and flip, and then

he has to do it all again.

Cheese gets the hat and brings it back,

and when he gives the hat to Mac,

Mac jumps for joy and shouts, “Oh boy!

How will I ever thank you, Cheese?”

And Cheese replies,

“Let’s close our eyes . . .

and just do nothing, please."